To Aaliyah and Marie

First published in the United Kingdom in 2002 by
The Chicken House, 2 Palmer Street, Frome, Somerset, UK BA11 1DS

Designed by Mandy Sherlicker.

Library of Congress Cataloging-in-Publication Data available.

ISBN 0-439-29658-7

10 9 8 7 6 5 4 3 2 1   02 03 04 05 06

Printed in Singapore

First American edition, April 2002

I Say a Little Prayer for You

Adapted from the original song by Burt Bacharach and Hal David

Illustrated by Karin Littlewood

The Chicken House

SCHOLASTIC INC.

New York

The moment I wake up,
before I put on my makeup...

I say a little prayer for you.

While combing my hair now,

and wondering what dress to wear now...

I say a little prayer for you.

Forever, forever you'll
stay in my heart,
and I will love you.
Forever and ever
we never will part.
Oh, how I'll love you.

Together, together, that's how it must be.

To live without you
would only mean heartbreak for me.

I run for the bus, dear.
While riding I think of us, dear...
I say a little prayer for you.

At work I just take time,
and all through my coffee break time...
I say a little prayer for you.

Forever, forever you'll stay in my heart, and I will love you.

Forever and ever we never will part. Oh, how I'll love you.

Together, together,
that's how it must be.
To live without you
would only mean
heartbreak for me.

I say a little
prayer for you.

I say a little prayer for you.

Forever, forever you'll stay in my heart,

and I will love you.

Forever and ever we never will part.

Oh, how I'll love you.

Together, together,
that's how it must be.

To live without you
would only mean heartbreak for me.

Answer my prayer.
You know every day
I say a little prayer.

I say a little prayer for you.